JUDY MOODY AND FRIENDS
Prank You Very Much

Megan McDonald

illustrated by Erwin Madrid
based on the characters
created by Peter H. Reynolds

CANDLEWICK PRESS

In memory of my dad

M. M.

To my sister-in-law, Huyền Lệ Kim

E. M.

Text copyright © 2020 by Megan McDonald
Illustrations copyright © 2020 by Peter H. Reynolds
Judy Moody font copyright © 2003 by Peter H. Reynolds

Judy Moody®. Judy Moody is a registered trademark of Candlewick Press, Inc.
Stink®. Stink is a registered trademark of Candlewick Press, Inc.

First edition 2020
An abbreviated version of this text appeared previously as "Judy Moody, Stink, and the Super-Sneaky Switcheroo" in *I Fooled You,* collected and edited by Johanna Hurwitz (Candlewick Press, 2010).

Library of Congress Catalog Card Number pending
ISBN 978-1-5362-0007-2 (hardcover)
ISBN 978-1-5362-0008-9 (paperback)

19 20 21 22 23 24 CCP 10 9 8 7 6 5 4 3 2 1

Printed in Shenzhen, Guangdong, China

This book was typeset in ITC Stone Informal.
The illustrations were created digitally.

Candlewick Press
99 Dover Street
Somerville, Massachusetts 02144

visit us at www.candlewick.com

CONTENTS

CHAPTER 1
Witches' Shoelaces

True or false? Judy Moody loved to play pranks. True! Judy had been playing tricks and jokes and pranks on Stink for as long as she could remember. For sure and absolute positive.

In the seven short years that Stink had been Judy's little brother, Judy had (a) fooled him with a fake moon rock, (b) tricked him into picking up a toad and becoming a member of the Toad Pee Club, and (c) freaked him out with the best-ever, fake-hand-in-the-toilet joke. No lie!

That was the long and short of it.
The A-B-C of it. She, Judy Moody,
Princess of Pranks, was in a mood.
A Prankenstein mood. A mood to
play a joke on Stink.

On her way home from her swim lesson, Judy tried to think of a brainy idea. Her best-ever-yet prank. She could not wait to say, "Prankenstein strikes again!"

When Judy got home, she did not hear karate chops in the living room. She did not hear zombie moans and groans coming from upstairs. She did not hear Stink in the basement getting ready for an asteroid.

"Where's Stink?" Judy asked Dad.

Dad looked up from his crossword puzzle. "He's out babysitting—"

"No fair!" cried Judy. "You said I'm not old enough to babysit yet, and Stink's younger than me. He's almost a baby himself."

"I was going to say, babysitting the tomato plants in the garden," said Dad.

Judy's face turned tomato-red. "Oh." She looked out the back door. "How much is he getting paid for babysitting tomatoes?"

"It's for the Summer Science Showdown," said Dad. "They hold a big event at the community center to encourage kids to learn about science. There's a torch-lighting ceremony, and everybody who enters a science experiment gets a gold medal."

"Stink was just telling us all about it," said Mom. "Let's see . . . Webster's building a tower out of straws that can hold a tennis ball, and Sophie is making a rubber-band catapult."

"It shoots mini marshmallows," said Dad.

"Rare!" said Judy. "But what is Stink doing for his project?"

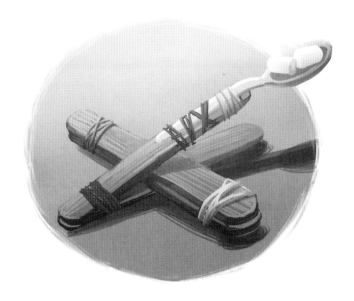

Dad shook his head. "Something about strangle weed?"

"And witches' shoelaces?" said Mom.

"Witches' shoelaces!" Judy ran outside to the garden. Stink had staked up three tomato plants with rulers.

"Wait. Is that my Women of Science ruler, Stink?" Judy asked.

"No way. It's just a thingy Mom uses to stir paint," said Stink.

Phew!

The tomato plants were already covered with teeny green tomatoes. "That was fast," said Judy. "These plants already have baby tomatoes?"

"But no red ones yet," said Stink.

"I wish they'd hurry up and grow."
Stink was on his knees. He had a
spray bottle in each hand. He was
sniffing all around the plants.

"What are you doing?" Judy asked.

"Shh!" said Stink. "I'm smelling."

"Hi, Smelling. I'm Judy. Nice to meet you."

"Hardee-har-har." Stink sniffed again. "Sniff right here. What do you smell?"

Judy took a whiff. "I smell dirt."

"You're no help," said Stink. "I'm trying to change the smell of the tomato plants. It's super scientific. I'm squirting the first row with this peppermint perfume I made."

"La Mint de Pepper. Ooh-la-la. Perfume with an attitude," said Judy. "You, too, can smell like a candy cane."

Stink chuckled.

"What's in the other bottle?" Judy asked.

"Pineapple juice," said Stink.

"At least it's not toilet water, like the last time you made perfume."

"I'm trying to get rid of dodders," said Stink.

"What's a dodder?" Judy asked.

"Let's just say there are no good dodders."

"I'm a good daughter," said Judy, cracking herself up. "Ask Mom and Dad."

"Not that kind of dodder," said
Stink. "A dodder is an evil weed. A
tangly, strangly vine that can actually
smell a tomato plant." Stink put his
hands around his neck, rolled his eyes
back, and stuck out his tongue.

"For real?"

"Science doesn't lie. When it smells a tomato, the dodder creeps up real sneaky-like and twists all over the tomato plant like spaghetti, then strangles it."

"Weird. So that's why they call it strangle weed?"

"Or witches' shoelaces," said Stink.

"Double cool!" said Judy. She looked down at her high-tops. Her own twisted shoelaces looked like a mess of spaghetti. Or a witch's tangled hair. Suddenly, her shoes felt a little too tight.

"It is so *not* cool," said Stink. "If dodders strangle these tomato plants, they'll die. I'll never grow even one red, ripe tomato."

"But just think—you'll grow a bunch of spaghetti plants. You could win the Summer *Spaghetti* Showdown."

"And flunk the Summer Science Showdown," said Stink. "My idea is that if I spray these plants with my peppermint perfume and pineapple juice, the evil dodders won't know they're tomato plants. April fool! They'll think it's a candy cane. Or a pineapple lollipop."

"So they'll be faked out and creep somewhere else?" asked Judy.

"Right."

"Wouldn't it be easier just to yank up all the witchy weeds?"

"This is way more scientific. Besides, they're super sneaky. They grow back fast."

Judy noticed a strangly vine that had twisted around her ankle. She wiggled her foot to shake it loose.

Stink held up both spray bottles. "You need my Dodder Busters." He double-barrel-squirted Judy's high-tops.

"Watch out!" Judy hopped out of the way.

"Now your feet will smell like a Hawaiian pizza!" said Stink.

Judy held out her left foot. "Hey! This one smells like mint toothpaste."

"You'll see. Pretty soon I'll be taking pictures of red, ripe monster tomatoes. Then I'll tell zillions of people at the Science Showdown how I saved these tomato plants. I'll be like some kind of superhero. Super Tomato Man to the rescue. They'll be better than any tomatoes you could ever buy at the supermarket," said Stink.

Judy was so in a pranking mood right now. And at this very minute, Stink, the best-ever brother to play pranks on, gave her an idea. A red, ripe idea. A dilly of an idea. A perfect pull-a-prank-on-Stink idea.

Prankenstein was back!

CHAPTER 2
Backyard Ninja Cat-Burglar Bandit

True or false? Judy Moody did not have a plan. False! She *did* have a plan. This was going to be the best fake-out ever! Her plan was to ask Mom to take her to the store. She had two things and two things only on her list: tomatoes and tape.

"Since when do you want to go to the supermarket?" Mom asked.

"Since now," said Judy. "I want to help out. Show you what a good daughter I am." Judy cracked herself up.

"No, really," said Mom.

Judy did some quick thinking and came up with an excuse. "We're, um, all out of frozen corn. And frozen peas for Mouse." Frozen corn was Judy's favorite after-swim snack. Frozen peas were her cat's favorite after-nap snack.

At the supermarket, Judy plopped
bags of frozen corn and peas into
the cart. Then she rushed over to the
tomatoes. "Mom, can we have tomato
sandwiches for lunch today? It's way
healthy. I know Stink is growing some,
but that could take all summer."

"Sure," said Mom. "Pick out a couple tomatoes and I'll grab the bread."

Judy knew which ones to get. The kind with green stems that looked like they had just come off the vine. She picked out two bunches.

"That's a lot of tomatoes," said Mom, eyeing Judy to see if she was up to something. But Judy just smiled

and said, "I really like tomatoes. It's my new thing."

She pointed down the next aisle. "And I need some tape."

"Don't you have a lot of duct tape at home?" Mom asked.

"I need the clear kind. It has to be see-through, not shiny," said Judy, trying to keep the mischief out of her voice.

As soon as Judy got home, she had to eat one and a half tomato sandwiches so Mom would not know she was up to something. She put the rest of the tomatoes in a bag. She hid the bag behind the cereal.

She, Judy Moody, was super sneaky. Terribly tricky! Perfectly pranky!

All she had to do now was wait until dark.

As soon as it started to get dark, Stink came in from Dirt Patrol (aka Dodder Duty). "There are monster mosquitoes as big as bats out there," said Stink.

"Better watch out for real bats, too," said Judy. "Vampire bats." Stink shivered. "I wouldn't go back outside tonight if I were you."

Stink shrugged. He went to the kitchen sink to wash his hands. He sniffed the air. "What's for dinner?"

"NOT tomatoes," said Judy.

Judy waited all through dinner. She waited all through dessert. She waited until Stink went upstairs to his room. She made sure Stink was way into drawing comics about Super Tomato Man and his sidekick, Ketchup Kid, before she made her move.

The time had come. The coast was
clear. Judy tiptoed across the hall to
her room and shut the door. Super
sneaky Judy dressed all in black, like
a ninja. She tiptoed back downstairs.

Terribly tricky Judy grabbed the supermarket tomatoes from behind the cereal. Flashlight?

Check.

Super-sticky see-through tape?

Check.

When nobody was looking, perfectly pranky Judy slipped out the back door into the night.

Stealing across the backyard on silent-cat feet, Judy headed straight for Stink's tomato garden. She was the Backyard Ninja Cat-Burglar Bandit, with only a flashlight to light her way.

CHAPTER 3
Prankenstein Strikes Again!

The next morning, Stink came running downstairs in his pajamas. His eyes were big. He was out of breath.
He pointed out the back window.
"You—look—see—my—Showdown—last—night—Dodder Busters—tomatoes—it worked!"

"Calm down, Super Tomato Man," said Judy.

"Take a breath, Stink," said Dad. "What are you trying to tell us?"

Stink gulped some air. "My tomatoes! Yesterday, all I had were puny little weeny green tomatoes. Then, presto whammo! All of a sudden my tomatoes turned red last night. Poof, just like that! Big, fat, red, ripe monster tomatoes. I'm a science genius!"

"Monster tomatoes?" said Judy. "Wow and double wow!"

"It's my Dodder Busters!" Stink pointed out the window again. "See for yourself!"

Mom and Dad and Judy went

to the window. The garden was
covered with red, ripe tomatoes! Mom
narrowed her eyes and looked right at
Judy. Judy put her finger to her lips.

"C'mon, Judy." Stink headed for the
back door. "Let's go see."

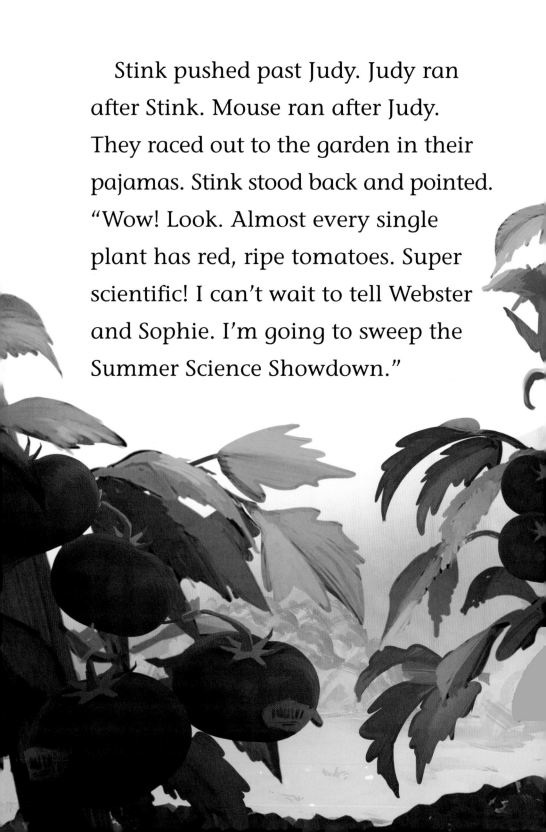

Stink pushed past Judy. Judy ran after Stink. Mouse ran after Judy. They raced out to the garden in their pajamas. Stink stood back and pointed. "Wow! Look. Almost every single plant has red, ripe tomatoes. Super scientific! I can't wait to tell Webster and Sophie. I'm going to sweep the Summer Science Showdown."

Just then, Mouse rubbed up against one of the tomato plants. Yikes! A red, ripe tomato fell off the plant. It plopped on the ground. Oops! Two more fell.

"Mouse! No!" shouted Judy.

Stink stopped. He squinted. He
stooped down to peer closer. "Hey,
wait a second. Something's funny.
As in fishy."

"Fishy? I don't see anything fishy.
Do you smell anything fishy, Mouse?"

"HEY!" Stink peered under a leaf. "These tomatoes aren't super scientific at all."

"Of course they are," said Judy. "Remember? They grew from teeny-weeny greeny ones to big, fat, red, ripe ones in one night!"

"Or did they?" asked Stink. He bent down to inspect the tomatoes up close. "These tomatoes didn't grow last night. Look right here. I think . . . that's . . . tape! Somebody did this. Somebody taped these red tomatoes onto my plants."

Judy had to think quickly to fool Stink. "I was trying to help you, Stink. Your tomatoes were so ripe they fell to the ground. So I, um, came out early and taped them back on this morning before you woke up. See? I'm not just a good daughter. I'm a good sister, too."

"Hold on," said Stink, picking up a tomato and turning it over in his hand. "These tomatoes have store stickers on them. This one says *organic,* and this one has a bar code. And this one says *Product of Mexico.*"

Judy Moody, the Princess of Pranks, aka Prankenstein, could not stand it one more minute. Not one more super-sneaky second. "Okay, okay. I did it, Stinker! It was me the whole time. I faked you out so bad!" she sang, jumping up and down. "Prankenstein strikes again!"

Stink looked like he was ready to pop.

Judy pointed at her little brother. "You should see your face. Your face is as red as a monster tomato!"

"I'm still going to sweep the Summer Science Showdown," said Stink. "But not for Dodder Busters. I'm going to win for my new invention."

"Your new invention?" asked Judy. "What's your new invention?"

Stink picked up all the supermarket tomatoes and collected them in the front of his pj shirt. Then he plopped a red, ripe tomato right on top of Judy's head.

Goosh! Slimy tomato goo slid down her face and yucky-blucky tomato juice dripped from her hair.

"Tomato shampoo!" said Stink. "I just invented it. Gives your hair that extra shine. And it's organic." A blob of tomato plopped on Judy's nose. She pulled tomato seeds and tomato goo from her hair.

Judy cracked up. "You got me good, Stinkerbell. You got me so good."

Stink grinned. "One good prank deserves another."

"Prank you very much," said Judy.
Stink held up another tomato.
"Super Tomato Man strikes again!"
True or false? She, Judy Moody,
ducked just in time.

True!